Go, Baby Jaguar!

adapted by Kirsten Larsen
based on the script by Chris Gifford
illustrated by Art Mawhinney

Ready-to-Read

SIMON SPOTLIGHT/NICK JR.
New York London Toronto Sydney

Based on the TV series *Go, Diego, Go!*™ as seen on Nick Jr.®

SIMON SPOTLIGHT
An imprint of Simon & Schuster Children's Publishing Division
1230 Avenue of the Americas, New York, New York 10020
© 2007 Viacom International Inc. All rights reserved. NICK JR., *Go, Diego, Go!*, and all related titles,
logos, and characters are trademarks of Viacom International Inc. All rights reserved,
including the right of reproduction in whole or in part in any form.
SIMON SPOTLIGHT, READY-TO-READ, and colophon are registered trademarks of Simon & Schuster, Inc.
Manufactured in the United States of America
6 8 10 9 7

Library of Congress Cataloging-in-Publication Data
Larsen, Kirsten.
Go, Baby Jaguar! / adapted by Kirsten Larsen ; based on the script by Chris Gifford ;
illustrated by Art Mawhinney. -- 1st ed.
p. cm. -- (Ready-to-read)
"Based on the TV series Go, Diego, Go! as seen on Nick Jr."
ISBN-13: 978-1-4169-4065-4
ISBN-10: 1-4169-4065-0
I. Gifford, Chris. II. Mawhinney, Art. III. Go, Diego, go! (Television program) IV. Title.
PZ7.L323817Go 2007
2006032335

Hi! I am Diego!

This is my friend

Baby Jaguar.

Baby Jaguar can run fast.

He can jump high.

He is great at climbing.

Baby Jaguar wants to climb to the top of Jaguar Mountain.

You can do it, Baby Jaguar!

Mama Jaguar is at the top.
Baby Jaguar wants to climb
to his mama.

Jaguar Mountain is not easy to climb.

It is very high.
There are many
big rocks.

Oh, no!

The rocks are falling.

Jump, Baby Jaguar!

Jump, jump, jump!

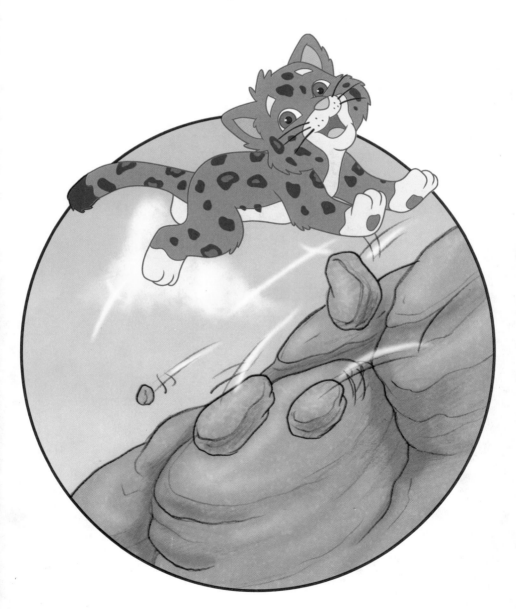

Jaguar Mountain is steep.

Climb, Baby Jaguar!

Climb, climb, climb!

We are almost at the top.

Run fast, Baby Jaguar!

Run, run, run!

Uh-oh! That is a big cliff.

Jump, Baby Jaguar!

Jump, jump, jump!

We made it to the top
of Jaguar Mountain!

Mama Jaguar is so proud.

Baby Jaguar is proud too.

Good job, Baby Jaguar!